WHAT'S LEFT ARE ECHOES

A novella by

GREG GILIA

© 2023 Greg Gilia

All Rights Reserved.

Reproduction or publication of any or all story elements recorded here without express written permission by the author, while flattering, is not cool, and would very much be frowned upon at the very least.

———

What else to do,
In this life so pretend,
But search on for you,
My dearest friend.

———

• • •

Thirty minutes pass for each and every trip from there to here, and from here to there just the same. Twice, daily, the safe transport of myself and my fellow degenerates is made to ensure our minds are trained and utilized appropriately in the areas of temporary memorization of specific dates, names, and uninteresting details of arbitrary events that do nothing more than feed an artificial sense of nationalistic pride. But it's quarter past three, and nearly everyone has been released from this yellow aluminum can of a vessel, like the parcels of trashy merchandise delivered from the factories and warehouses operated by the slave-like workers that we are gradually being trained to become.

Next stop is mine, just around this next bend. The forest green gives way to a wide open field, and a gravel driveway leading up to the house at the top of the hill with Charlie, my dog, sitting patiently halfway up the slope. The school bus comes to a stop and I see

Charlie perk up a bit, now standing up on all fours, looking forward to greeting me. What a great guy. Even at his age, with arthritic hips and a bit of a limp, he's still just as eager and excited to see me today as he was last year, or three years ago, or ten years even, when he was just a puppy. Just as excited to see me as I am to see him.

I stand and look up ahead to where my younger sister Scarlett sits. She grabs her things in an armful and walks awkwardly down the aisle, holding her jacket and bag tight to her chest while making no eye contact with anyone she passes by. I follow behind her and step off our prison coach to make my way back home to Charlie. Scarlett walks ahead up the driveway and Charlie rushes down, making a beeline straight for her. Dropping her things with little concern of their condition, she opens her arms wide for Charlie's embrace, just like she did last year, or three years ago, or ten years ago even, when Charlie was just a puppy. Except this time Scarlett isn't really there, no matter how clearly I see her. Charlie passes right through her, almost as if intentionally aiming for the same delirium-induced mirage that infects my reality, but he passes her by and buries his head into me in the purest form of love and affection, and I do the same. This is the moment I'm alive for. Another day thrown away without my consent to gossip and boredom finally leading up to a moment's embrace of appreciation and love. But a moment is all there is for the good things before they are disrupted by the unending bad—in this case, the nauseating shouts of a loveless marriage escaping the loosely insulated walls of an old farmhouse.

The obnoxious noise of stress and hatred catches our ears, causing both me and Charlie to look towards the house in the direction of the clash of bickering, but it's a reactionary glance without thought. It's been far too long for there to be any compassion left for these people who want so badly to make the other miserable, regardless of who gets caught in the crossfire. So, just like every other ineffective solution to all of life's other problems, I look for distraction, as is the way of my species. Tossing my bag to the side of the driveway, we decide it's best not to head inside quite yet.

"Come on, boy," I say to the only joy in my life, and we head together into the woods to cling tightly to this brief moment in time before it gets pulled forcibly away by the setting sun of another day.

We head into the woods together, just like we've done together thousands of times over the years. Charlie makes sure to be a few steps ahead, as usual, confidently leading the way. Not as many steps ahead as he used to be in his younger years, but still not one to drag himself behind.

The steep slope just beyond the forest's edge leads to a valley, and nestled in it is an old, dilapidated cabin that was apparently lived in by the original owners of this land before the house we live in was built. You can see it from up here at the top. As I begin to descend, there is a movement that catches my eye, but I'm not deceived by it this time because I've seen it several times recently from this same exact spot. Just another hallucinatory reflection of the way things used to be. It's Scarlett, climbing up the aging, cracked logs that line the outside wall of the cabin—up and into a window opening that leads to the upper loft. It's a climb we've made many times together in our hideout of sorts, even though Mom and Dad forbade us from ever going near it out of fear of a collapse. Since she disappeared I've seen her climb up that wall many times. And each time I saw her I would run after her, climbing up and into the same opening that we did many times before, but each time I do she's not really there. I would wonder to myself if she ran away and just lived out the year hiding in the old cabin, sneaking away from me whenever I attempt to seek her out, or if she died and her spirit just had nowhere better to go, but it has since become more obvious as time goes on that a third explanation seems the most likely: I'm losing my fucking mind.

Even though I see her so clearly, Charlie doesn't seem to pay much attention to her, so I choose to do the same. He may be old, but he's sharp. Sharp and sane. A lot more than me, anyway.

We head down the hill, but not all the way down. Just to the halfway point. It's here where a long rope hangs from a tree branch high up, tied at the bottom end with a handhold loop. Another thing we used to do as kids—we'd grab hold of this rope and lunge off of the edge of the incline, swooping out and around, soaring through the air by two hands gripped to a forty-foot rope before the momentum pulls us back inward to where our toes touch the ground.

Arriving at the rope, though, it is already in motion. Swinging out and in as gusts of wind push and ease up against my back. I say gusts of wind because that's how I can rationalize it. In truth, I see her here too. Just as I saw her at the cabin climbing the outer wall, I see her here swinging out over the edge and coming back in for a landing, disappearing from existence as I grab hold of the rope on its way back in. I fear that openly admitting to myself what I see will only lead me deeper into this broken state of consciousness. Visions of her have been getting more frequent as time goes on, and I certainly don't want to accelerate this state of mental decay any faster.

I used to assume that what I saw were ghosts. The spirit form of my sister coming back home. But why? Why doesn't she communicate? Why doesn't she tell me what happened? Why would she even be here at all when she could just as easily be exploring the infinite wonders of the cosmos? The reality of it is that these are nothing but reflections of her life created by me—by what I know of her. My mind is telling me she is here because my mind is broken. Because I am broken. I know that now, but even knowing it doesn't make it go away.

Gripping the loop with both hands, I take a running leap to propel myself off the side of the hill, swinging freely and letting my mind temporarily float away with my body before landing back on the ground and doing it again. Again and again, with each swing farther out than the one before, and with each landing becoming more at ease.

After pausing for a second to collect myself, I grip the rope tight again in preparation for another swing when a brief flash of imagery overwhelms my vision—a glimpse of a rope swung over a tree branch against a darkened night sky. Choosing to ignore the unwanted imagery and the tinge of sudden anxiety that accompanies it, I lunge off the side of the hill to forget it all away, which is the closest thing to a solution that I've discovered so far. But then, as I reach the farthest point outward before being pulled back— the point where the body and mind feels most weightless and unattached from the world—another glimpse bombards me, this one more clear than the one before. It is my sister's face. Struggling, choking, suffocating in distress. She convulses and thrashes wildly in so much pain. It's so vivid that I can feel it myself, so I lose grip and fall to the hillside below, rolling uncontrollably down the steep incline. Pummeled by stumps and hardened soil on the way down like angry fists, then finally coming to a stop before long. Charlie must've rushed down behind me because just as soon as the tumbling subsided I felt a gentle nudge telling me to look up from my face-down position—up at Charlie poking his nose at me to see if I'm all right.

Physically I am, but still I cry uncontrollably, wheezing and choking in what I think is despair.

I don't know what happened to Scarlett, and I don't know what's happening to me, but I know I have Charlie, so I grab hold of him tightly, shivering and burying my tears into his neck. He doesn't mind. In fact, he knows this is exactly what I need right now.

• • •

The night finally comes and I spend it as I usually do: struggling to comprehend my own thoughts, with Charlie sprawled out on the bed beside me, and a pair of headphones drowning out the stern tones interspaced by shouts from the unhappily married couple that occupy the room below mine.

It's so hard to think sometimes. Hard to understand the waves of thoughts that splash and collide against one another in my head. It's weird how thoughts work. All scrambled up, messy. Just figuring out what one of your own thoughts means to you is like putting together a thousand-piece puzzle with no border, and where all of the pieces are singular, solid colors that change depending on the angle you view them at. Just as soon as you find a place where a piece fits, it soon becomes apparent that it just as well belongs somewhere else entirely.

That's why we ignore them, I guess. We distract ourselves from ourselves with other people's lives. Gossip, fiction, social media. Or we fixate on a singular emotion—one that we can understand as it's portrayed in its most basic form through story or song. We use drugs and alcohol, an endless supply of pornographic fantasies, empty friendships—all to distract from what we fear and don't understand.

It used to be so much easier, though. So easy to escape my mind I didn't even realize I was doing it. Maybe that's the problem. Maybe now there's just too much to hide from, and I've been hiding for so long that I never learned how to face any of it. Now the options that remain are to either numb my mind further with greater distraction, or let this confusion and anxiety consume me fully, allowing myself to free fall into the depths of madness.

Why don't they teach us this shit in school? How to fucking think. How to fucking process thoughts in a way that allows us to actually use them. Maybe writing it all out will help. Maybe I can capture my thoughts as they come, put them on paper and then converse back at them before they warp into other piles of nonsense.

I wonder if that's how others decipher their thoughts, or if most people even try to figure them out at all. That's what Scarlett did, I think. She was always writing. More than she talked, anyway. Maybe she was on to something. Laying out the things that confuse you, confronting them head-on instead of ignoring them. I'm so tired of being confused. I'm so tired of being scared and alone.

Fuck. I'm already starting to sound like Scarlett. Who knows, maybe I'll disappear too. Fingers crossed.

THUD! THUD! THUD! The sounds of knocking disturbs the hypnotic instrumental rhythm pouring out of my headphones and disrupts my thoughts before they're given the chance to take the shape of anything tangible. So I take off my headphones and hear the pattern repeat, this time accompanied by a muffled voice from outside my bedroom door.

"Open up, Mira," my mother commands. "We have to talk."

"It's open," I say, and the door creaks open obnoxiously slow before my mother cautiously steps in and takes a seat on the bed beside me.

"What are you guys fighting about now?" I ask, as if I'm the one that summoned this meeting between the two of us.

"We weren't fighting, we were just talking—and I'm not here to talk about that. I came to ask you why you've been skipping school again," she states with the unreserved efficiency of completing a routine chore at the end of an uninteresting to-do list.

"I didn't," I so eloquently respond. Which was true about today, at least.

"Don't lie to me," she snaps back, but I saw that one coming so I snap back just as fast.

"You lied first."

It's dumb, and I'm sure we both know it. Two living things that speak the same language and live under the same roof, yet entirely unable to converse in any worthwhile way. But meaningful conversation isn't really our goal here. She is here to confront me about the problems I care little about, all the while ignoring the obvious problems that affect the whole family.

"I'm sorry, Mira, I really am. I'm not lying to you, I just have a lot to figure out and it's been hard. If you want to talk about that then sure, let's do it."

"About you guys getting a divorce?" I ask, hoping it'll help to rip the band-aid off. In reality it just made things noticeably more awkward and difficult.

"If I were to move out..." she pauses between thoughts, "...if I were to find another place—an apartment for the two of us—would you be okay with that? Both of us leaving the house and not living with Dad anymore?"

"Me leave?" I ask, surprised that the default option for me is to leave my home behind. "Charlie would hate living in an apartment in town. He's used to it here. He loves it here," I remind her, spewing my rational concerns that somehow got overlooked.

"Just you and me, I mean. Charlie would still be here. He won't be bothered at all," she says, as if talking to a child not yet capable of having their own rationalized observations.

"I'm not leaving Charlie just because you want to leave. Whatever you want to do is fine, but I'm staying here."

"Mira, you can't base your life around the dog. I'm serious here. If I were to leave would you choose to stay here and live with your father?" She pushes further, as if there's something I'm not understanding.

"I'm staying with Charlie. I don't know why that's so surprising."

It's true that I don't get along well with Dad, at least not since Scarlett disappeared. He was so unloving...so mean to her. Once Mom and Dad started fighting things immediately fell apart and Scarlett got even more distant than she already was. And then she ran away. Killed herself, most likely, but who knows. No body, no trace. Maybe she's out there somewhere living it up. Maybe it was her in the cabin that I saw and she's just really good at hiding. Or maybe she hung herself like the visions in my mind insist.

I can see my mother holding back tears while still sitting on the edge of the bed, and she stops herself before saying another word, knowing that the words will turn to sobs, so she silently rises and walks to the door. Through a saddened voice she mutters a reminder that I am to miss no more school, and then steps out into the hall, closing the door behind her where she quietly breaks down, helplessly afraid, confused, and alone. I know exactly how she feels.

Charlie lifts his head up, looking concerned by the sounds subtly heard from beyond the door. "It's okay, buddy," I remind him, "it's me and you, and I won't let anybody change that."

• • •

I don't remember falling asleep, and I'm not sure how I slept through my alarm, but I wake up to faint sounds of barking coming from outside. Out the window I see a deer in the distance disappearing into the tree line, and Charlie hobbling along after it. He may be old but he still loves a good chase when the opportunity presents itself. I know he can't keep up with it, but there's no telling how far he'll go, so I call his name out the window. Knowing it'll go unacknowledged, I rush downstairs. Dad is obviously gone already because he usually lets Charlie out when he leaves in the morning. I throw my shoes on—no time to tie them—and burst out the back door, ignoring the questioning shouts from Mom, still in her room, as I run out.

I head for the trees where I saw the deer enter, and call out Charlie's name at the top of my lungs. I call but see no response, so I run even faster. I dash into the trees, getting nervous about how far ahead he may already be by now, but then I see him standing there looking back at me. He looks off in the distance, likely in the direction the deer ran, and then back to me as if I'm at all interested in following the deer.

"Come on, Charlie. Fuck, you scared me, buddy," I say, and he comes to my side with no hesitation. Just a little adventure to pass the time but, damn, it scared me.

"Scarlett ran off a year ago, I don't need you to go running off now too."

We head back for the house and I see the school bus taking off down the road, passing by my empty driveway. At least it's not really my fault this time.

Back at the house it's clear that Mom isn't happy.

"Charlie ran after a deer," I tell her, "so I missed the bus."

"I don't want to hear excuses. I don't have time for it," she says.

"It's fine," I reply, "I can catch up tomorrow. I'll just stay home today," which really wasn't my initial plan but works for me.

"Get in the car. I'm driving you," she commands, and so I comply.

As the car pulls out of the driveway I can already tell it's going to be a tense ride. Mom looks disturbed. She remains silent and looks straight ahead as if extremely focused on driving, but her mind is noticeably elsewhere.

Someone on a bike is up ahead hogging the side of the road, yet Mom seems to pay them no mind. She speeds straight ahead without hesitation, approaching dangerously close. I clench the armrest of my seat, and just as I'm about to blurt out a confused warning I realize it's Scarlett that I see. We zip by close enough to confirm it is indeed her. Close enough to see the tears streaming down her face as she rides alone. Close enough to see that she wasn't really there.

"Do you ever see ghosts, Mom? Like, someone that isn't there but it looks as if they are?" I ask, and immediately regret.

"Please, Mira. I can't deal with this right now," she dismissively responds. Of course she doesn't want to deal with this right now. Neither do I. Except I don't have the choice.

"Sorry," I say. "I know she's gone, but I just keep seeing Scarlett everywhere, but then she's not really there."

"You don't know she's gone, Mira. We can't think like that," she says, albeit unconvincingly.

"Then why did they stop the search for her? Don't you think they came to some sort of conclusion by now?"

"No, Mira, I don't. I think that's just what they do. They look for a while and then they stop until they get more information. She ran away and she's always been good at hiding." Mom adjusts her posture and seems to make an effort to humor me a little, remembering suddenly to try to pretend to care about what might be going on outside of her own little world for a change. "Besides," she continues, "if you keep seeing her, isn't that proof that she's still out there keeping an eye on her big sister? What's she doing, anyway—when you see her, I mean?"

"On her bike with her backpack, just now. She was biking down the road. We just passed her," I reply, knowing exactly how crazy it sounds.

Mom glances in the rearview mirror to confirm to herself that nobody was there, and then glances at me sympathetically, as if that's what I'm looking for out of this. Honestly, though, opening up a bit about my crazed delusions did seem to lighten the otherwise tense car ride, for better or worse.

"Why did Dad hate her so much?" I ask after a moment of silence while trying unsuccessfully to think of a smoother segue into the question.

"He didn't hate her, he just..." she pauses, "... we all make mistakes, and sometimes those mistakes aren't something we can take back."

"The 'mistake' being Scarlett?"

"No, not Scarlett. Your dad and I have had issues getting along sometimes, even back when you could barely talk. After a few too many pointless arguments, I had spent some time with a good friend of ours and, well, your father was never the same after that. He never trusted me. He never trusted that Scarlett was really his daughter. I mean, biologically." She tenses up and grips the wheel, and I see her eyes begin to water. I can feel it in the air that she's ashamed and embarrassed to be talking to me about this right now.

"Is she?" I ask without hesitation.

"No," she answers as bluntly as the question was asked, and the tears roll down. "He's known that for a while now," she continues, "but I made the mistake of keeping it from him for far too long. He would bring it up all the time, assume I was lying, like I couldn't be trusted. And I guess he was right about that. He didn't hate Scarlett, he just hated what she reminded him of, and sometimes he couldn't handle it. He always loved her, I know that's true, but it was hard for him to show it. I don't know if it was his fault for not showing her the love she deserved, or my fault

23

for bringing her into this mess, but we both screwed up, and now we both lost her."

"No, we all lost her," I feel the need to remind her, which of course just causes her to break down even more. But she's not mad, and she manages to hold it in after a few minutes.

"What else is she doing when you see her?" she prods a little more, noticeably trying to fill the emotional silence with conversation.

This talk of my sister begins to open my mother up to listening more sincerely, and speaking without anger in her voice, but her question just reminds me of the horrifying visions I try so hard to forget. They flash in my mind only briefly, but they come to me as clearly as they did yesterday while swinging on the rope with Charlie. I see her choking. Struggling to breathe. I can't get it out of my head and I don't want to keep it to myself anymore, so I tell her.

"Dying," I reply.

Mom looks back at the road as I look back out the window to avoid the sight of her renewed stream of tears, and we drive on in uneasy silence.

• • •

Minutes feel like hours when I'm at school, and yet at the end of the day it was all just a blur. Another day wasted to tedium, and now I'm back on the bus departing for home.

I rarely ever see her at school—visions of her, I mean. I wonder why. It's distracting, it's noisy. Maybe I just don't notice her there. Maybe she blends into the background like she did when she was still around.

Where was she going this morning on her bike, I wonder. Riding down the road with her backpack stretched full. There's nothing out that way, just fields and trees. Town is miles away, and she never biked to town, at least not that I know of anyway. More importantly, why do I even believe these things that I see when I know logically that they are imaginary? Do you only become insane when you allow yourself to believe in that which isn't real? And, if so, does that mean if I ignore it it'll all go away eventually?

I jot down these thoughts and it makes me realize that all of my beliefs are just questions I haven't found answers to yet, rather than actual legitimate findings on anything. I see something that doesn't make sense so I question it. It consumes my thoughts because I find no definitive explanation better fitting than what the question implies, and then it etches itself more permanently into place the longer it lingers without a legitimate answer, so I complacently accept the unfounded assumption as real. I wonder how much of the way that I view the world is entirely wrong simply because of this lazy thought process.

Rather abruptly, as the bus approaches a stoplight downtown, I feel my mind drift, and my observations no longer matter as more haunting imagery rips through whatever thought I was just clinging to. I see what appears to be a man in a mask that covers the lower half of his face. He's looking down at someone on a cold, clinical tabletop, but I just barely see him, as if through a haze. Or more like a silhouette in bright, blinding light, and then the image is gone entirely as I feel the rumble of the bus accelerating from the stoplight that just turned green, prompting me to put down my notebook and pop on my headphones to distract my wandering thoughts.

It does the job, because after what feels like only moments later I open my eyes to the school bus stopped at the end of my driveway with the door opened up waiting for my departure. I scramble to grab my things and rush off, somewhat flustered by my own inattention.

Heading up the driveway I feel a little shaken up. It seems like even when I'm not totally out of my mind I'm still not all that grounded. I let these thoughts and feelings overwhelm me too much, and then I purposely disconnect from myself because I can't handle the anxiety. I fear that facing them will pull me in deeper and I may never escape, though, conversely, I fear ignoring them will preserve this never-ending juggle between profound confusion and purposeful disconnect from reality. God, is this all I have to think about from now until the day I die? It seems so shallow yet insurmountable.

Scarlett was seeing a shrink before she disappeared. Fourteen years old and already facing what very well could have been the same issues I'm having now. They drugged her up and she got weird. Not *bad* weird, but *different* weird. Now she's gone. Realistically, she probably wasn't having the same problems as I am, at least I hope not. I don't know what she was going through, really, but I know she didn't fit in. Not just at school—that was normal for her—but at home, too. She acted as if she was an unwelcome guest unable to leave. Barely speaking with my mom, and not even accidental eye contact with my dad. He really seemed like he hated her, and we both could tell. I didn't care though, she was in her own little world and I had my own problems to deal with. Except those problems don't matter anymore, and now she is all that I think about. Her and Charlie —speaking of which, what the hell?

I rush up to the house after a lengthy driveway stroll without ever having been greeted by that big lovable face of his. I pop my head in the door and see Mom sitting at the dining room table with her laptop out.

"Where's Charlie?" I ask.

"He wasn't outside?" she questions in response.

"No, he's normally waiting for me but he wasn't there today. Where did you see him last?"

"That deer he was after...I think he saw it again. I heard him barking earlier," she says calmly, as if everything's fine.

"What? How long ago? Why didn't you go get him?" I shout, as confused as I am angry.

"Mira, that dog is always after something. I can't watch over him twenty-four hours a day." Her words fade away as I head back outside to look for Charlie.

I run back to where he entered the woods this morning, thinking that he would probably just hang around where he saw it last.

"Charlie!" I scream, and follow it up with an attempted whistle. "Charlie, come on boy!"

I see no trace of him here and I feel a crushing hopelessness hit me all at once, like I am weak and lost, and have no idea what to do next. So I keep running, and as I run I alternate between airy whistles and loud shouts of his name. I run deep into the trees until I'm out of breath, and only then I realize that this was just a guess, and he could really have headed in any other direction just the same. But this isn't like him. He wanders a bit, chases things away from the house, but he doesn't lose himself like this. Where would he have gone?

A sense of dread comes over me and I feel paralyzed. I don't know what else to do but keep calling out. Eventually my screams and whistles grow quieter as they give way to weeping that I have no control over.

It must be hours that have passed, and it's just me sitting on the forest floor alone. The sun is going down and Charlie is nowhere to be seen. I pick myself up and head back home, hoping desperately that Charlie is waiting there for me when I return.

The house is dim when I enter. Mom must be in the bedroom while Dad sits alone in the living room with a bottle of beer that likely isn't his first.

"Have you seen Charlie?" I call to my dad.

"I haven't seen him. Your mom says he ran off," he responds, inattentively, with his eyes fixed to the television screen. "What's wrong with you?" he adds after a glance in my direction, taking notice of my puffy, red eyes.

"What do you think? You don't even care that Charlie ran off? You don't even care to help me find him?"

"I went looking for him when I got home— looked for both of you. Your mom said Charlie was gone and you must've went looking for him. You didn't hear me calling? I'm sorry, Mira, but sometimes you can't do much but wait," he explained in his usual apathetic tone.

"Like with Scarlett? Just wait around and hope she comes back? 'Cause that sure seemed to work," as if I needed to remind him. "Or was that the idea all along? Mom is always complaining about Charlie so it's no surprise she did nothing to call him back home when she was the only one here. And it doesn't seem like you stuck at it for too long either."

"Mira, please," he interrupts.

"Please what? Please disappear and stop bothering you? Please run off into the woods like Charlie, away from a home that doesn't care? Please kill myself like Scarlett so you no longer have to be burdened by my existence?"

"Stop it, Mira!" he shouts back. "I didn't say that," he continues more sternly, "you know that's not what I said. And don't talk about your sister like that, you know that's not what happened."

"No, I don't know that, Dad. I don't know anything about what happened. I know you hated her, and that you treated her like shit because she wasn't really yours, and then she disappeared. That's what I know, and it's just the same with Charlie. You guys can hate each other all you want but it's everyone else that seems to suffer. It's no wonder everyone tries to escape here. I guess I'm the dumb one for still hanging around," I say through my anger and frustration, keeping surprisingly intact through it all. Normally I'm a wreck when it comes to any type of confrontation.

"Who told you that about your sister?" he asks, knowing it can't be refuted.

"Mom told me, but it's not like it wasn't obvious."

"Just stop, Mira. Maybe you should just go to your bedroom. That seems to work fine for your mother," he says, and turns back to stare blankly at the soulless visual stimulation on the screen in front of him.

A football game is on and he uses it as a crutch. Alcohol to numb his mind, and TV to distract, just like everyone else. Not that it matters. There's no point talking to him so I storm off to my room alone. No Charlie, no Scarlett. A mother and father who barely speak to one another. The only thing clear to me is that what little remains of this family has deteriorated beyond repair.

$\mathbf{\bullet}\ \mathbf{\bullet}\ \mathbf{\bullet}$

I wake up the next morning with tears in my eyes, having dreamt of the worst outcome for Charlie, and of course he's not here to console me when I wake. Just his scattered clumps of fur resting on the side of the bed where he sleeps. I push the memories of my dream aside in hopes that it quickly becomes forgotten, as most dreams do. Unfortunately for me, that is a fate most commonly reserved for only the good dreams.

Out the window I hear no dog barking but I look anyway, and it is then that I see him staring into the forest's edge just like the day before. Unlike the day before, he's not really there. It's nothing but a wishful thought mixed with a memory played out on repeat before slowly fading away. The reality that's left behind reveals no sign of him.

I rush downstairs to see if he turned up over night, hoping to myself that he's lying outside the door waiting for someone to let him in, but he's not there either.

"You're going to be late again," my mother says from the kitchen when I poke my head out the front door.

"CHARLIE!" I call, in case he's around.

"I'm serious, Mirabel. You can't miss school again today," she continues, ignored and unacknowledged once more.

I close the door for a moment and put my shoes on.

"Where are you going?" she asks, already knowing the answer.

"I'm going to find Charlie. He's still out there."

"He'll come on his own if he didn't go off and get himself killed. You're not going to find him out there looking around without a clue, and you can't afford to miss more school," she rambles on, unsympathetically, as I do my best to drown out the sound of her.

"Mirabel," she continues sternly, "the bus will be here shortly and you're not missing it."

"I'm not leaving Charlie out there alone any longer. I'm not just going to stop looking for him like you stopped looking for Scarlett," I blurt back.

"Nobody stopped looking for Scarlett!" she shouts. "There's only so much control we have over situations like these. I called animal control, and if anybody sees him it's them that will be the first to find out. They'll call us as soon as something comes up."

"I'm going to look for him," I persist.

"I don't ask much of you, Mirabel, and God knows there's little I expect. But I'm telling you you're getting on that bus or so help me God I will have that dog put down when he does show up for all the trouble he causes."

"What is wrong with you! How can you care so little about everyone but yourself?" I ask, more sincerely than she could possibly understand.

"I do care, Mira. I care about you more than anything. That's why I'm worried about how much school you've been missing, and how much you will regret it when you're supposed to be graduating but instead still stuck here catching up. I worry about your priorities, and about who will help you with them if you were to live alone with your father. I worry about losing both of my daughters, so the least I can do is be a mother while I'm able to. Please, just go to school today and try to get your mind off things. I'll call around to the neighbors and I'll keep my eyes peeled for him, I promise," she says wholeheartedly. Deep down I know it is of little use to roam hundreds of acres of wilderness blindly in search of him. He knows where home is, but I can't help but think he got hurt out there. People around here treat an animal on their property as they would an armed intruder. Everybody's just looking for an excuse to pull a trigger, but I guess if she calls around at least that's a good first step, so I reluctantly obey her wishes, pack my things, and head down the driveway to wait for the bus.

It arrives, unfortunately, so off I go on another wasted day of note-taking and forgettable facts under the guise of intellectual development while stressing unavoidably over the whereabouts of my best friend and companion. At least that's what I would've expected to be in store for me, except on the way there I have a sort of déjà vu in the form of a vision of a man in a surgical mask—possibly the same man I glimpsed yesterday on this same street in town not far from the school. Still submerged in blinding white light, however, this time I make out a syringe in his hand as he looks down at his victim, hovering above the hard, flat surface where they rest. Resembling a doctor, but the whole thing instills a dreadfully helpless feeling to my core. Did this man do something to Scarlett?

I exit the bus along with everyone else when it pulls in to the school drop-off lot, but rather than heading inside, I make my way down Main Street to quench this irrational yet inescapable beckoning I feel that draws me to this specific location. Where this location is exactly, I'm not sure, but it's not long before I arrive at a doorstep with a sense of certainty that this is it. My heart sinks deep inside and I feel like I need to vomit, but I know I have to face what's in front of me to see for myself if there is any truth to this madness.

I step inside the door and walk up to the reception desk of our family's veterinary clinic and, with barely a thought, I ask for the paperwork from the last visit of my dog.

"Yes, certainly, sweetheart. Your mom was in yesterday with him. I'm so sorry for the loss…he was such a great dog. I guess he'd been having fits of seizures that have been getting out of hand, your mom said, so it was just his time," the receptionist says with a practiced sympathy in her voice.

It all comes as a shock and I can't hold back the tears. I clench my stomach with both hands and cry out uncontrollably in deep, sobbing breaths as horrific, irrepressible thoughts pummel my emotions. My friend, my brother, my escape—Charlie's life was taken, and it was by my own mother. My mom is a liar. She knew he's the only happiness I have left and she took him from me. For what? Because my love for him is real, and my love for her is nothing but an instinctual obligation? Because I cared more to stay with him than to flee from Dad with her? What is wrong with them? Why is everyone so fucking insane?

"I'm so sorry, dear," the receptionist repeats, and she comes around the counter to give me a hug, as if the gentle touch of a hired killer could be any form of consolation. I can't stand it, I have to get out of this place that took Charlie's life so willingly. I have to get out of this town that drags me down so mercilessly to their level of moral abandonment. I have to get away from the murderous monsters that lie to me and take from me what matters most.

Nothing in this world makes sense to me anymore except for the madness that won't leave me alone. And now, it seems, that's all I have left.

• • •

I spent the day under the Main Street bridge in a form of shock while waiting alone for time to pass before I could get back on the bus to head home. Not that I wanted to go home, it's just that I had nowhere else to go, and I knew I needed to confront my mother about what she did to Charlie. Being betrayed so severely by the person you've been taught to trust your whole life is a feeling that little else compares to. It's like an entire world collapsing in on itself without warning and without end. Just a perpetual state of rage, panic, and confusion. A literal end of the world would be less traumatizing because it would at least be a shared pain that can be seen and understood, and would soon grants us with the inevitable release from our mass suffering.

This is something else entirely. It is a lethal crime without justice, committed by someone I once trusted against someone I love more than anything else in the world. It strikes deep into my soul and I tremble to the bone. Alone, lost, and forsaken.

What is the word for that unbearable feeling when you've lost everything imaginable and there is no getting it back? Is it one that has been excessively misused and watered down, like most other truly poignant words, to the point where it reaches nowhere near the impact it was originally intended to have? Is there even a word for this at all, or do the people who have experienced it just end their lives before ever having assigned a word to its meaning?

I questioned throughout the day if I should go home at all. What would it solve? What am I expecting to achieve? Maybe I should just never return; disappear like Scarlett.

No, I don't want to give them that satisfaction. Disappearing without them ever knowing why, allowing them to defensively assume it was by no fault of their own. I have to go back. I have to tell them that I know what they did, and I have to make sure they understand it was them that killed Charlie, it was them that killed Scarlett, and it was them that killed everything that is left of me.

• • •

It has been a day of confusion and inner turmoil. On top of that, being questioned by friends—or people on my bus that I happen to know, to put it more accurately—about my whereabouts as of late, but not in a concerned enough manner that they pay any mind to the evasiveness of the hollow responses I deliver.

Over the past year I've become the weird kid at school, but nobody really bothers me about it all that much because they feel bad about my sister or something. She was the weird kid before, back when I was the normal one. That's the way it always used to be. Except they weren't as indifferent towards her about it so she got just as much verbal abuse at school as she did at home. For which I wasn't much help, to be honest.

It's like she didn't care enough about the people around her to try to change in order to become accepted by them, and I guess I understand that sentiment now. If anything, I've learned to respect that about her. In a way I kind of always did, I just didn't realize it then.

In any case, the bus ride goes by with as much pent-up stress and rage as you could imagine. Conversations played out in my head repeatedly, each with mild variations in how I would approach my parents. None of them ended well, but there's really no happy ending to be salvaged here.

I get off the bus and drag myself up the driveway like an exhausted mountaineer low on oxygen and food supplies, all the while whispering loudly to myself the words that are playing out in my head like a true psychotic, screaming at my mother in mumbled breaths and hearing her responses as if they were spoken out loud.

Standing outside of the house, I can't bring myself to enter. Everything has changed, just like it did when Scarlett disappeared, but this time I know exactly who to blame, and somehow that only makes things worse. When you know the truth there is no choice but to face it. When you don't know then you at least have an opportunity to keep hoping for the best. But what good is hope if there is no truth to it? Is a life that revolves around lies and uncertainty worth living any more than a life of devastating honesty? I knew that knowing the truth could hurt far worse, and yet there is nothing I wanted more than to know, so apparently there is more value in truth than there is in the bliss of the unknown.

One thing is for certain: I'm sick of the lies and I'm sick of the liars.

Still standing outside the house, the conversation fades from my mind and I'm left with nothing but debilitating pain, confusion, and anger. I hate them so much and I don't know how to tell them.

A rock the size of my clenching fists rests by my feet. I pick it up, as if instinctually, and succumb to the urge to throw it as hard as I possibly can through the window of my parent's bedroom. The glass doesn't stand a chance against the force of the throw, and the rock strikes clean through like a bolt of lightning accompanied by a thunderous crash that pierces the air. I hear my mother's surprised scream from inside the house, then I see her face peak through the hole in the broken glass.

"What the hell are you doing!" she calls out in angered bewilderment.

"FUCK YOU!" I scream back, entirely off script from all of the variations of this confrontation that played out in my head throughout the day.

Through the shattered glass and the darkness of her bedroom, I see in her eyes the look of regret that I'd imagine any killer would have upon being caught.

She knows now that I know, but she doesn't yet want to believe it.

I don't make a move to step inside, and she doesn't make a move to come out. We're at a standstill, and neither of us know what to do next. It's a long silence but I have to push on. I have to know.

"Why did you kill him?" I cry out. "What did he do to you? What did I do for you to take him from me?"

Mom steps away from the window, walking slowly back out of her room. I stood trembling in silence without noticing the gravel crunching under the tires of my dad's truck until the squealing brakes force it to a stop right behind me, and then I hear the slamming of the door after the engine shuts off.

"What happened?" he asks at the sight of me standing in tears in front of a shattered glass window.

"Did you know, Dad?" I sincerely want to know.

"Know what? What happened?"

"Mom killed him. Mom took Charlie to the vet and had him put down for no fucking reason."

"Baby girl," he whispers as he rushes over to hug me, but I push away.

"Did you know?" I repeat as firmly as I can before my words turn to emotional, incoherent mumbling through quivered lips. "Were you part of this, Dad? Did you know? Did you? Did you fucking know?" I mumble on while pushing away more aggressively at his physical attempts to console me.

"No, I have no idea what's going on right now," he pleads, "how do you know this?"

"Because I saw it in a dream and it was real," I begin to explain, but he interrupts with condescending doubt.

"Mira..."

"No, Dad, I saw it and it happened. I went to the vet and they told me everything. Mom said he ran away but he didn't. She took him to the vet and..." I can barely continue. I hunch down into a ball, hugging my shins and burying my head between my knees while a stream of tears drips down my legs. I feel my dad standing beside me not knowing what to do, and then the sound of the front door opening. Glancing up, I see my mom standing in the doorway looking devastated, as if it were her that is the victim here.

I can't bear sitting here waiting for them to speak more lies, just as I can't stand to look at them, so I get up and burst into the house, pushing past my mother on the way in, then rush up to my room to get away from them. I have no words left, only tears, and

I don't want to share them with those monsters, so I cry alone into a pillow facedown on my bed.

• • •

I didn't sleep all night. How could I? I just laid there cycling through thoughts and memories. Memories of my own, and memories of others that feel as if they were my own. I can't explain how, but I saw fragments of the events leading up to Charlie being killed. I felt his fear, his confusion. It felt like it was happening to me even though I wasn't there to experience it.

What is this madness that reveals truth? Is it all just coincidence? Mom always says there is no such thing as coincidence, but I know that's not true, like most things she says. Just another empty statement—a flawed belief that acts as an answer to bizarre occurrences that really doesn't answer anything at all. Maybe this is all just a coincidence. Or maybe, in this instance, I'm using my belief in coincidence as an answer that really doesn't answer anything at all.

Flashes of memories churn in my mind as small bits solidify and take shape into greater clarity. The vet holding the syringe. Charlie's tense repulsion to being held firmly in place against his will. Scarlett climbing into the cabin. Biking down the road. Choking. Gasping for air.

In this moment of reflection I lie still and focus on the images that haunt me. I let them in for a change, rather than trying to suppress them as I normally would. Recalled visions play back one after another in no consistent order, and each time I feel a little more connected to them.

I begin remembering other encounters of unwanted thoughts that I managed to forget. I see Scarlett standing in the hall outside of my parent's bedroom late at night, listening as they argue. She must've found out about Dad back then and had nobody to talk to about it. I remember her trying to confide in me, but I had no patience for her. She would ask if I had a minute, of which I had plenty, but none I ever spent on her.

It keeps playing back, each time more vivid than the last. I get up from bed and step into the hall where it took place, and now I'm watching it unfold in front of my eyes as if it were all happening right now for the first time. Scarlett stands outside their door, eavesdropping while they talk about her. Dad screaming at Mom about our old neighbor Sam, and about how Scarlett is a constant reminder of him. Mom crying back that he is looking for excuses to act the way he does. Asking him if things would really all be better off if Scarlett was never born at all. Accusing him that he acts as if he'd rather she be dead.

Scarlett hears enough for it to all be too much. She knocks on my door, and I hear myself tell her to leave me alone. And I never see her again.

Am I making this stuff up? Looking for connections to explain away my own mental illness, or am I seeing things as they were—as I was never able to see them at the time?

My notebook fills with recounted memories that don't belong to me, and with back and forth attempts to make sense of them. At this point, though, there is only so much wondering one can do without getting lost in endless circles. There is only so much isolation and self pity before giving in to total, inescapable depression. That sinking feeling of having nothing to live for—I hate it, but in a way it's good because when you have nothing left to lose, the truths that remain hidden are no longer frightening to reveal. It's so hard to look for truth because it feels so much more comfortable to ignore it all, just like I used to do with my visions. But I'm no longer comfortable, and have no reasons left to keep on ignoring.

I saw visions of truth as if they came from Charlie. As greater clarity emerged, it was as if I was outside of him looking in. I am haunted by apparitions that I believed were of my own making, but today I realize that I'm not the one that is mad. I'm surrounded by people that deceive, lie, and kill. They will forever continue to convince themselves that their actions were for the best because that's what makes them most comfortable. For those looking, though, the truth is there to be found, hidden behind the noise and confusion, calling out to a crowd of people too distracted—too entertained—to hear it. Finally, now I'm listening.

I spend several hours of the night in deep meditation recalling memories of Scarlett. The images grow more pronounced as I focus in on them, but it becomes hard to tell if I'm elaborating on these events with my own imagination or if they are actually revealing more of themselves to me. I fear that forcing this state of mind may replace truth with more fictitious nonsense. It's hard to grasp what is truly an intervention from the great beyond, and what is constructed by my own psychological unraveling. The difference between the starring role in The Bible and a ticket to the psychiatric ward just comes down to a popularity contest, after all.

It's not like I believe that I am chosen by some godly being. I just think a part of my sister remains, like Charlie, and can tell me what happened. She's been showing me all this time, but just like when we were kids, I turned her away.

I won't do that anymore, though. Now I take in what she's saying, no matter how hard it is to accept. She shows me the same memories over and over again, and each time I become more attentive to them. And as I become more attentive, a little bit more of the memory is revealed.

I watch her again overhearing my parents fighting about her as she stands in the hall outside their bedroom. I watch her again approach my room and knock on my door with nobody else to turn to. And she is rejected, just as I saw before, but she doesn't disappear from my sight this time. More of her story unfolds as I see her walk away after my door closes shut in refusal of her plea for help. She walks back to her bedroom, so I follow. There I see her packing her things, slamming clothes and books into her backpack hastily, slowing down only for brief moments to wipe away tears. I walk up to her hoping to touch her, but when I reach out she is gone. She fades away, hiding the rest of her actions from me. And then, in a flash, I see her for another brief moment—not in her room packing her things, but deep inside my mind, appearing drenched in a darkened sky, showing me again her last gasps of air before leaving this world.

Over and over again her suffering flickers through my mind, with each replay extended by milliseconds longer than the one prior, but still feeling so distant and hard to grasp. Eventually I see words come out of her mouth, but I can't make them out. It's like she's screaming to me from a soundproof space. And then, finally, I hear it. Nothing else except for one word. The only word I needed to hear, "—Dad," cried out right before a rope tightens around her neck.

I can't take it anymore. Everything in my world is collapsing in on itself and I just want it to end. As I leave Scarlett's room I'm bombarded in the hall by more visions. I see Charlie run past me and into my room as if to check on me, which he's done many times in the past. I see Scarlett hunched down against the wall at the end of the hall crying alone. I turn to look at the other end of the hall and she's there too, but this time she is much younger. Happy and dancing around all excitedly until something startles her and she runs off into her bedroom. None of it makes any sense. It's all disjointed and chaotic.

I walk down the hall and quietly open the door to my parent's room. It's late and the lights are out. They don't hear me come in and I'd rather keep it that way.

In their closet is a metal lockbox that is never actually locked. It's just protected by a hanging rod full of shirts that droop down in front of it. The closet door is already open, so all I have to do is quietly reach through the clothes, lift open the rigid door of the lockbox, and there it is. I reach in and pull out my dad's loaded 9mm pistol and a spare clip—a weapon I've handled a few times before when Dad was teaching me about gun safety. I double check that it's loaded and then release the safety before making my way over to their bed.

My hands are shaking and I can barely keep myself together. More visions flood my mind, this time of Scarlett sneaking into Dad's wallet on the nightstand beside their bed, and then the look of regret on her face when she hears someone coming in. Movement catches the corner of my eye and I see my grandfather walk by the doorway, looking in as he passes, as he's done hundreds of times back when he used to live with us before passing away.

My reality feels as if it's drowning in moments of the past. I can tell they aren't physically here when I see them, but they're becoming so much more visible that I don't know how much longer I'll be able to distinguish the real from the mirage. Focus, Mira. Focus and end this.

I raise the gun and aim it towards the left side of the bed only to realize my father isn't there. Mom squirms and starts to roll over, so I throw my arm behind my back in a panic to hide the gun.

"Michael?" She murmurs.

"Where is he? Where did Dad go?" I ask, wishing they were both here together.

"Mira? What are you doing up? Can we talk now?"

"Where's Dad?" I repeat. I have no desire to speak with her and it would only make things worse.

"He went out, maybe for the night. I'm sure he'll be back in the morning. Can you just sit down and talk to me now?"

With the gun still behind my back, I grip it firmly, and lightly touch my finger to the trigger. It's hard to resist what I want to do to her right now, but I can't risk Dad coming home before I find him, and having him see what I have done.

I carefully slide the gun into the waistband of my pants and flip my shirt over top before leaving the room in a rush. In the hall I see multiples of Scarlett, all in different stages of life. I can't handle any of it right now. I just have to get out of here, so I run for the front door. Once opened, Charlie's there waiting to come in. I burst into tears and collapse on top of him but land on my hands and knees just outside the door with no Charlie in sight. Why is this happening to me?

I begin to crawl across the gravel driveway until slowly rising back up to my feet to make my way to Mom's car parked on the other side; keys stored carelessly in the driver's side cup holder, as usual. My uncle lives in a duplex in town a couple of blocks from Main Street. That's where Dad always goes when they're fighting too much. To escape from his problems, I guess, but he won't escape from what he did to Scarlett. And Mom—I'll be back for her, too. Soon it'll all be over.

did to Scarlett. And Mom—I'll be back for her, too. Soon it'll all be over.

$$\bullet \bullet \bullet$$

I start the engine of my mother's hatchback, nervously put it into gear, and drive down the road. Up ahead of me I see Scarlett riding her bike exactly where I saw her last time when Mom drove me to school.

It takes me about half the amount of time it should normally take to reach the turn that leads into town, and as I begin to pull left on the wheel, I see Scarlett, again on her bike, but she's not turning towards town. Instead, she's continuing on straight, which doesn't really lead anywhere other than an old gas station and convenience store twenty minutes ahead. I haven't been that way in ages.

Deciding instead to follow Scarlett's tracks, I swerve abruptly back into the lane and carry on straight ahead in that direction. She soon fades away, as she always does, but not before giving me that much-needed breadcrumb to follow.

After about ten minutes, I pass by the old gas station and convenience store. Our old house isn't far from here—where we grew up before moving to the farmhouse—and all of a sudden pieces of the puzzle begin fitting together differently in my mind. I make a right turn off the main road where the moonlight becomes shrouded by dense foliage. Even in the darkness everything is so familiar here: the winding dirt road, the scattered cherry trees, the old barns in the distance barely managing to hold themselves up. It's all so comforting, like going back in time to when things were all right.

Finally, I see the house I'm looking for, which turns out to be more of a trailer fixed atop a concrete foundation. I never realized how modest it all was when we were here last, but I guess I didn't really have anything to compare it to back then.

I park the car on the side of the road just past the driveway, and cautiously approach the house. Empty beer bottles are stacked up on the porch, and old car parts decorate the lawn. It's a pretty standard sight out here. Two steps up a pair of creaky, rotting boards that bend from the weight of my foot leads up to the front door, but I hesitate to knock. Sliding my palm against the handle of the gun that's still fixed behind me, snug against my waist, I slide my index finger over the trigger in preparation, but then pause for a long moment before walking back down the steps. There's something out here I need to be sure of first.

Around the back there's plenty more rusted scrap metal, car engines, worn-out tires, and everything else you'd expect to find in a hoarder's paradise. Beyond that, though, is the missing piece I've wondered about all this time. Right there in front of me in the form of a tall, twisted tree standing alone on a grassy hilltop. I can't stand the sight of it. Haunting to look upon, and instilling a sickening sensation, as if it were the place of my own dreadful memories.

It's agonizing to be here. It feels as if I'm swinging back and forth from the branches of that tree with a rope around my neck. I feel it squeezing tightly and I can't breathe. Down on my knees I bow to the ground, as if too weak to stand, and I do my best to take in slow, deep breaths that feel blocked and constrained by my own windpipe, and then I look up and see her. After another struggled gasp I race up the hill to reach her, but my stomach sinks and my body feels like lead. This unbearable torment I feel that grows with each step as I approach the tree and look on helplessly at my sister swinging left and right, clawing at the rope around her neck, and kicking her feet downward in an attempt to gain footing on nothing but air.

The closer I get, the harder she struggles, and worst of all, I know I've already failed her. I know that as soon as I reach her she will be gone. And, sure enough, she vanishes before my eyes as I fall to the ground below where she died.

The grass is patchy here. More sparse in one spot than the rest, like it has been dug up at some point. After tossing the gun to the ground, I claw into the soil with my fingers and rip clumps of earth from where I kneel. I dig like a dog, nails tearing from my fingertips, and clothes soaking in filth. I dig and I don't stop. Several feet down now, I just keep digging. I dig through the physical pain, and then through the numbness that follows. I dig until finally I can see her for real, lying beneath the soil in a state of decay. I touch her with my cracked and bleeding fingertips, and I brush away the dirt on her face. Remnants of flesh still sticks to her skull but there is not much left. She is comprised of worms as much as she is of human tissue at this point, but at least I finally found her. Exactly where she brought me.

•••

Within a torn, mud-soaked knapsack by Scarlett's side is a tattered notebook, but it contains no words. The pages are soaked through and stuck together. Whatever thoughts that were recorded within it are no longer legible. Decayed away like the rest of her, except for the images of her past that revealed themselves to me.

I can't help but cry, and through my tears I thank Scarlett for staying with me all this time. I thank her for giving me the strength to do what must be done. And with that, I brush away the loose dirt scattered atop the gun that had dropped to the ground before I began digging. Squeezing it firmly, I head back to the front yard and up the creaky steps to the entrance.

Scarlett appears to follow close behind. I see her come up the steps from down the driveway after dropping her bike to the ground. I watch her as she walks right by me, knocks on the door, and enters. I do the same, but nobody answers, so I bang harder, and harder still. Then, with barely a pause, I turn the unlocked knob and let myself in.

The last time I was in this house was when I was nine years old. Scarlett was even younger. I don't remember it being quite this messy back then, though. The dishes are piled up at the sink, empty beer bottles scattered around. A cigarette in an ashtray by the couch, still lit. Next to it, a window overlooking the tree where I found Scarlett. He could've been watching me dig her up this whole time.

There's Scarlett again, standing just inside the door asking if she could spend the night. Pleading to her father for help, "Sam, I'm not sure if you remember me," I faintly hear her say, "I grew up down the street and I wanted to see you."

I say I heard her, but that's not exactly accurate. It's like I felt the words within me, and they are translated in my mind as her voice being spoken. It's all the same, really.

I felt so strongly it was Dad that did this to her, but all this time it was her biological father that was to blame. But why?

I walk over to her, and as I do she fades away only to reappear on the couch beside where I just stood. She's tired—falling asleep on the couch. Before she does, though, I feel her call out to him. "Sam," she says, "can you come sit with me? I don't want to be alone."

Scarlett fades away again while whispers of her words echo in my head, "I need you, Sam. You're all I have." The words are faint and overlapping each other, but I'm able to make them out so much easier now than I was before. "He knows he's not my real dad. I know that now too," Scarlett's conversations of the past continue. "You are, Sam, and I need you so much. I just need somebody."

Suddenly the words are interrupted by sounds of thudding and crashing, but in this focused state I'm in I can't tell whether it is current or from the past.

"SAM!" I call out, and readjust my hand to maintain a firm grip on the gun. I begin walking to the bedroom, and as I do I hear more crashing and banging, and I see the closed door to the room vibrate with a violent force like someone is trying to break out. The weird thing is that the actual door isn't really shaking at all. I see it as a hazy overlay, like a hallucinatory replica of a door on top of another, but only for an instant before everything is returned to an unnerving calm.

Nervous, scared, and shaking from adrenaline, I reach out and place my hand on the door, take a deep breath, and then turn the handle. The door opens slowly to the sight of my sister constrained on the floor, choking, with a rope around her neck. She cries out apologetically, as if this were all her fault. I feel her words as I watch her try to force them out, "I'm sorry," she gasps. "I just wanted to know you, Dad," her plea for understanding continues before being silenced by a tightening noose as it drags her violently across the floor, sliding helplessly past me with muted screams out the door I had just opened. I don't even reach out to her. I just close my eyes and wait for the past to end, and then it is silent again.

On the bed sits Sam—the real Sam, I mean—with a drink in his hand, and darkened, bloodshot eyes that paint a picture of his current state of being. The sight of him startles me and I instantly forget how to move or speak.

"I didn't know she was my daughter," he forces out as tears fill his eyes. "She came over, asked to spend the night. I didn't know what she wanted—I didn't know why she was here." There is a long pause as he tries to catch his breath and wipe away the stream from his eyes, and I can tell he's trying to speak but keeps choking up. I grip the gun with both hands and point it at his chest, and then he continues, "I thought it was me she wanted. I thought she came for me, but really she just came for my money. Accusing me of being her father after she settled in here. I thought she wanted me, not just my money," he sobs.

"What fucking money? She came looking for her father," I shout through quivering lips; my whole body trembling more than ever.

"I thought she wanted something else. I made a mistake," he reiterates.

"You killed her! You tied her up and hung her, and for what? Because you thought she wanted to fuck you, you sick fuck! She's my little sister and you took her from me, you pathetic piece of shit!"

Sam gets up from the bed and takes a step toward me. I feel frozen stiff but still trembling. I just want to run but I'm not capable of it. He steps closer, walking right up to me without ever making eye contact. With eyes fixed on the gun, he reaches out and pulls it from my hands. I didn't even try to resist, it's like I just gave it to him. Maybe this is what I wanted. Maybe this is the easiest way to get back to Scarlett and Charlie.

Finally he looks at me, right into my eyes, and I see a weak, pathetic man. I see a lonely man capable of love, like anyone else, but never knew where to find it. I see desperation and regret. I see confusion and sadness. I see everyone I've ever met in the eyes of this man, and I hate them all.

I close my eyes and wait for him to do to me what he did to my sister. I look forward to it. Fuck him, and fuck this world that creates people like him. I'm so sick of it all.

"Tell your mother I'm sorry," are his final words before the deafening gunshot reverberates through the hollow walls of his bedroom, and I hear him fall hard to the floor. My eyes open up to see his body convulsing in a puddle of blood that grows larger by the second. I can tell he's still alive and suffering, but only for a few seconds more. Nowhere near as long as it took Scarlett.

I feel his blood on my face, dripping down and soaking through my clothes. I smell it with every breath. I can't stay in here any longer, not with him, so I stumble lightheadedly through the house to make my way back outside. I can't handle any of it—my sister's body in the backyard, Sam's in the house. I don't know what to do right now so I just run. I run down the road just like when I was little. A mile away, maybe two, I run until I get home—our old home, back when things were good. It's the same mailbox, the same cedar fence, the same sky-blue front door. I miss it all so much.

I sit on the porch and look out at the yard for what must've been hours before the sun appears to brighten the morning sky. I watch the birds in the cherry tree and the bees in the flowers. I sit silently and watch, and then I cry. I cry and I don't stop crying.

The door to the house opens, startling me from behind, and I hear a voice call out, "what happened—are you okay?" but I can't say anything, all I can do is cry.

Before long, a pulsing red and blue hue shines through the dense foliage that lines the dirt road, and a cruiser pulls into the driveway.

"It's okay," I hear an officer say, "we're going to get you home." Words spoken to bring comfort and safety, but they mean nothing to me.

• • •   • • •

Memories are all we have left from the events of our past. Thoughts and feelings; imagery that encapsulates the way things used to be. Unfortunately, memories are also imperfect and incomplete. They are one-sided, and easily altered by personal bias. Your own memories are anyway. Fortunately, that's not all we have. We have their memories, too. Memories lingering from others, like ghosts trapped in this world, except non-sentient, and thus unwavering against the weight of desire.

Memories of the dead don't remain here for some contrived purpose of haunting those who have wronged them, or to play practical jokes on descendants of their bloodline as if they were children never getting bored of the same silly prank. How horrifying a thought that would be, becoming trapped in this world after death, unable to be understood or felt, with the only form of communication being the mysterious creaks and knocks of an old house at nighttime. But no, there is no reason to fear a fate such as that, for we are not the ghosts we leave behind. They are merely fragments of what we once were, dissipating slowly over time, as everything does.

What are we other than biological mechanisms to create and transmit thoughts? And what are thoughts other than organized data compiled together to be accessed and understood as long as that data remains intact? Without the mechanism to create, there is no sentience, there is only data. And much like the information traveling around the world to and from our phones and computers, the data of the mind communicates wirelessly, too, throughout the interconnected web of all living things.

We create thoughts, and those thoughts drift along in a captive state, like waves of pure information capable of being received by other receptive minds. Much like our physical form, thoughts, too, inevitably succumb to their own slow decay, naturally relinquishing their energy like a ripple mellowing in time, giving way to an empty canvas of calm for new forces to flourish.

In a way, it's beautiful—knowing that the thoughts of others are out there waiting to be received. New perspectives to be gained from those that were perhaps unable to communicate them verbally during their time spent among the living. They can be felt, seen, heard, and understood long after the biological entity that formed them turns back to soil. They can inspire new thoughts in minds still capable of rumination, and then, in a way, living on even longer than a fading thought could otherwise last.

We are our memories, and our memories live on beyond our physical form for at least a while longer, but most of them are feared or ignored by the still-living. We block them out with distractions, unintentionally severing a vital connection to the past, distancing ourselves from ourselves with each societal and technological step forward. It's all so backwards and absurd, but that is our way. At least, that's how I've come to look at it.

These are the current answers I've reached since embarking on this journey of thought exploration, deciphering my own no differently than I do the thoughts of others. Perhaps one day my thoughts will be received by someone else able to expand on them further, and understand them even better than I do in this moment.

Though I haven't seen Scarlett since the night that I found her body, other voices have reached me on occasion, and more do still to this day. The less of a connection I have to them, the more distant their thoughts are to mine. But we are all connected, it's just a matter of tuning in to the right frequency, blocking out the interference, and listening wholeheartedly.

I never did go back home the night I found Scarlett. I refused. I had no reason to go back, and legally I wasn't a child anymore. A chapter of my life had ended that night, and it was up to me to force the next one to begin.

It's been years now since I left home. Haven't seen either of my parents since. I went from a troubled outcast on a farm to a traveling street urchin. Out of desperation I became a beggar. Out of fear I became a liar. Out of despair I became an addict. The medication they put me on allowed me to lose sight of my visions. The drugs I took by my own accord, though enlightening at first, soon resulted in a dependency that pulled me further away from my own thoughts. But, much like the chapter that came before it, I ran from that life too. I fled deep into forests still unscathed by man, and high into the mountains above his watchful eye. I've searched for the wisdom of fellow travelers, many whose lives ended before my journey even began, watching and learning from teachers unknown to anyone alive today. And now I think I'm finally ready to listen to everything I once refused to hear. I'm ready to go back home.

That's where I'm headed now as I sit in the passenger seat next to a stranger kind enough to drive me the hour-long distance from the train station in exchange for forty dollars. The ride is silent but not awkwardly so, mainly because I've kept my nose in these old notebooks the whole time, revisiting the past on my way to revisit the past.

"It's just up here on the left," I say as we pass a familiar bend right before the dense forest gives way to a wide open field that reveals a For Sale sign at the bottom of the driveway. I can't help but feel nostalgic by the sight of the old house on the hill, with a balanced mix of excitement and discomfort.

A sticker exclaiming "REDUCED" is plastered over top of the sale sign in bold lettering. Leave it to my parents to ask for far more than what it's worth, and reduce it begrudgingly as if they're the ones being ripped off.

The car pulls up the driveway and comes to a stop. No words are spoken for a moment while we both gaze upon my requested destination.

I heard it was for sale a while back. Emptied out, move-in ready. It wasn't long after I left that Mom and Dad must've finally went through with the divorce. It was probably Dad that stayed living here the longest, and no doubt put up a fight to not have to sell the land. Nevertheless, neither of them are keeping it, that much is clear. It looks nearly unlivable now with old, damaged shingles exposing patches of rotting wood on the roof, and stucco crumbling off the exterior wall. I would think the house has seen better days, though, in hindsight, it was never much of a sight to behold.

"So is this your house or something?" my chauffeur wonders out loud to me.

"Yeah, I grew up here," I respond. "Just taking care of a few last things before it sells."

"Need help with your bags?" he asks while popping the trunk open with the press of a button, not so subtly hinting that his job here is done. "No," I say, "you've already helped enough. Thank you," and I exit the car, grab my bags from the back, and knock twice after closing it shut to confirm the end of our transaction.

Long after the car drives off I stay standing outside, gazing at the house in front of me while trying to stave off the emotions I felt that day when I tossed a rock clean through the window, which has since been replaced. The way I felt back then is rekindled almost instantly upon peeking in through the window of the front door that reveals the house, though empty, exactly as I remember it. The rage and desperation I felt, the artificial love, the constant ridicule, the lies and deceit—it's all coming back to me just as it was back then. I turn the handle and push, but it's locked from inside. Of course it is, but I jiggle harder, then begin to pound on the door with one hand still twisting the knob. Slamming my fist against the wooden surface, then kicking it with my foot until the worn, cracked wood holding the latch in place on the inside gives way, and the door swings open. I didn't plan on breaking and entering, but here we are.

It's dark inside, and more quiet than I have ever known it to be. Plates resting decoratively on exposed cupboard shelves, clean oven mitts hanging perfectly centered on the handle of the oven door. On the counter is a welcoming bowl of wrapped candies, like the kind you would find at your grandparent's house as a kid. All just subtle messages left by the real estate agent, subliminally grasping for your attention like a ghost from the past. How fitting.

It's odd, the rage I feel while standing in this place. Everything that I told myself I wouldn't feel is exactly what is enveloping me. I don't know what I was looking for, really. Closure of some sort, but I'm not even sure as to what. Memories flash before me of the screaming and the anger between an ill-fitted family. I'm reminded of that deep feeling of isolation in a house full of people, but these are all memories I've seen and felt before. These are my memories, playing back to me from my own mind as they have always been. I'm not sure there is any further insight to be gained by coming back here. It's just more of the same noise to wade through that kept me distracted all those years, and took me so long to release.

I close the door behind me and walk slowly down the hall and up the stairs, working my way straight for Scarlett's room.

I've been in here many times since Scarlett left. It feels a bit different now—emptier, and with a fresh coat of paint. It's a weird feeling being in here without her things. It's almost like seeing it as it is now is making me forget what it was before. There is nothing in here of hers. It's as if she never existed at all.

Through the sadness of loss that washes over me, my anger still grows. The thought of forgetting Scarlett, how insulting that would be to her, and how rewarding that would be to my parents. Imagine that, the stain you've left behind being wiped clean, freeing you of the guilt that you so deserve.

I can't stand the thought of these people and the weight they have on me. It's them that should be forgotten.

Leaving Scarlett's room behind, I make my way back downstairs and into my parent's bedroom.

Not quite as empty, with the master bedroom being a key focal point of house viewings, I assume. A bed remains here with the headboard perfectly centered against the wall. It's their same bed, left behind, unwanted by either one of them. The memories seeped into it must be better off forgotten. Beside it sits another artifact of their past in the form of a bedside table that probably hasn't moved from that spot since the day we moved in. Looking around, there is not much else of note, but I feel the need to walk over and touch the wooden surface of the tabletop, as it is one of the few remnants from my youth that is still here, however insignificant it may be.

I slide my hand across its surface, and down to the decorative handle of its upper drawer. Then I pull.

Inside is nothing but an old photo album, either staged or unwanted while clearing out the house. It's an old one, and I vaguely remember flipping through it as a kid. Baby photos, toddler shots, and lots of random pictures from the house we lived in before this one. There are even some more recent ones taken here on the farm. Flipping through I see one of Scarlett and I kissing Charlie on the cheeks from each side, sandwiching him with our love. I'm going to keep that one.

Further ahead I see Mom and Dad with big smiles and holding hands. I see birthdays and trips to the lake. I see us as the family I never remembered. I see Dad holding Scarlett in his arms with the sort of loving embrace that can't be faked. I see Mom and I reading side-by-side next to a campfire. I see love.

I blurt out an audible choke trying to hold back tears, but who am I really hiding them from?

They begin to stream down my face and I just let it all out. The pain of what once was, and of what it eventually became. The misery I brought upon all of them by dwelling on the ways they've wronged me. The sinking feeling that the end of this family was as much my doing as it was theirs. I don't forgive them, but I know now that I'm just as much to blame.

Look at me, look at what I have to offer this world. Is all that I have to leave behind just a portrait of confusion and disdain? No hope or guidance? No reason for being?

If you have nothing to offer those that seek you out other than darkness, it is then that you become the demons lurking within nightmares. Just another jaded voice pulling the bright-eyed ones into the same depths of despair that you yourself never managed to escape.

If you have no love to leave behind—if all you have to give back to this world is more pain, why stay any longer at all? Why allow it to fester and grow?

Jolting me from my thoughts of self loathing is the sound of the front door slamming open and shut from strong gusts of wind pounding against it. As I look up to the doorway of my parent's bedroom leading out to the hall where the slamming sounds rumble through the hollow, empty space, I catch a glimpse of a figure hurrying past.

It moves in the direction of the source of the disturbance down the hall, and as it does I hear the sounds of sadness echoing throughout the house, like sobbing coming from all directions. At first it is faint, but it grows louder the closer I get to the figure while I follow behind it towards the front door.

Still scurrying ahead of me, just out of reach, the figure in the darkness ahead disappears outside as the door slams shut behind it from the pounding wind.

The wind dies down soon after, and the door remains shut, as if closed tight by the ghostly apparition escaping my presence, but I know it was just the result of wind blowing against a door with a damaged latch. After all, I broke it myself. But I also know I saw someone—a figure in the dark. She was right there in front of me, so close, like looking at my own shadow.

I reach for the door but hesitate to pull it open. Can I really endure more pain from the forgotten memories of the past? Aren't my own tormented emotions enough for me?

I can't help but contemplate the thought that putting an end to this journey entirely and joining the masses on their path of self-suppression seems the better way. Go back to school to prove I'm as borderline functional at basic math and geography as everyone else. Get a job that makes me hate the weekdays just enough to grant a small dose of pleasure at the arrival of the weekend. Get married to someone I find mildly attractive so that we can invest a large quantity of our mental energy on convincing ourselves why we should remain together over the years as our love inevitably fades. Retire from a job that I hated only to realize that I've conditioned myself to do nothing else, leaving nothing but purposeless boredom for my remaining years of declining health.

"No," I say out loud to myself, "I would rather the pain and loneliness of truth," so I reach back for the handle and pull the door open, and then I see her. Kneeled down in front of me, the crying girl that ran outside from the hell of this household, except she's not crying anymore. She's happy. As happy as anyone could possibly be. I know that for certain because it is myself that I glimpse upon. Standing in the doorway, looking down at a reflection of my own past from years ago. A moment in time still lingering, waiting to be shared with others who happen upon it.

I look down at her and feel the same comfort I can see in her as all of her problems melt away in an instant. Knelt down with arms wrapped tightly around the purest joy in her life.

Charlie buries his head deep into my arms to comfort and console, as was his way, and I watch myself burry my head into his neck and squeeze tight to take it all in, just as I always did. Even though I know it is only an image of what once was, it is an image that has not yet faded, reflecting back to me a glimpse of our past no differently than the view of the sun arriving as if with us in the same moment, when in fact it is nothing more than a transmission from over eight minutes in the past. Yet still it gives us warmth. Still it gives us comfort. Still it gives us truth. And still it guides us on our way.

It appears to me as though the present moment is something that barely even exists in our lives. It leaves just as soon as it arrives, but in the wake of one moment, the story of a lifetime remains for many moments more, bouncing back at those who choose to see. Our experiences that are transmitted outward are delayed messages sent from moments of the past, like the light from the sun, or packets of digital data sent to and from electronic devices. We are but senders and receivers of thought, born from one moment to be experienced in the moments that come. What's here right now is the creator of thought, what's left are echoes waiting to be heard.

WHAT'S LEFT ARE ECHOES

A novella by

GREG GILIA

www.ingramcontent.com/pod-product-compliance
Lightning Source LLC
Chambersburg PA
CBHW020748160726
47993CB00006B/2661